Paul Rogers
Forget-Me-Not

Illustrated by
Celia Berridge

KESTREL BOOKS / LONDON

THE VIKING PRESS / NEW YORK

Sidney's in a dreadful state.
Unless he hurries, he'll be late.
He's off to visit Cousin Joe.
There's so much to remember though!

The present's wrapped, the card's been done,
A fishing rod – that might be fun,
Binoculars, to see the view,
A towel could be useful too.

Raincoat, hat, umbrella, snack,
Thermos, camera, key and pack:
He's made a list of everything,
But which does he forget to bring?

Sidney's bus soon comes along.
He takes a seat, but something's wrong.
Jumping up, he cries: 'Oh dear!
My umbrella isn't here!'

Off he gets to catch his train,
Look – it's just begun to rain.
He goes to put his raincoat on –
Now where on earth could that have gone?

Never mind: he's caught the train.
Time to check his list again.
'Oh no,' he sighs, 'it can't be true.
I've lost my brand-new Thermos too!'

Fields and farmyards rattle past.
Here is Sidney's stop at last.
'The sun!' he cries. 'Just look at that!
Did I forget to bring my hat?'

Sidney's only halfway there.
Now he has an hour to spare.
'Time to fish,' he thinks. 'That's odd,
I'm sure I brought my fishing rod.'

'Still,' he says. 'What's done is done.
I think I'll picnic in the sun.
Just a minute, though. How weird,
Now my snack has disappeared.'

NEXT
BOAT
TRIP
TO THE
LIGHTHOUSE
3 PM

Time to go and get the boat.
In he climbs and off they float.
'I need a towel. The seat's all wet.
Now did I have one? I forget.'

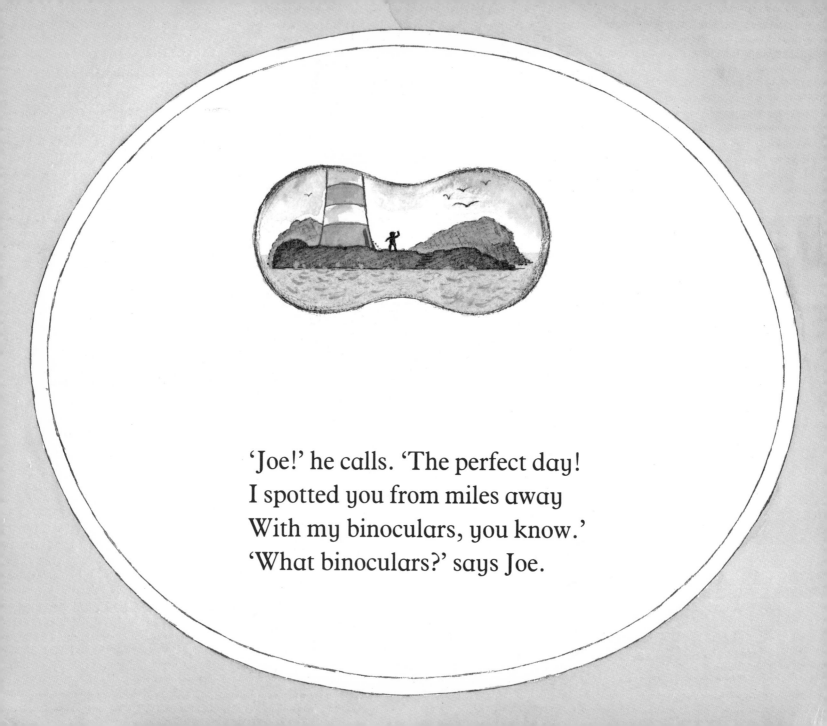

'Joe!' he calls. 'The perfect day!
I spotted you from miles away
With my binoculars, you know.'
'What binoculars?' says Joe.

'I've lost a few things on the way,
But not this gift, I'm glad to say.
Happy birthday! It's a cake.
But where's the card for goodness' sake?'

'Bye,' he says at last. 'But no.
A photo just before I go.
Hold on, my camera isn't here.'
'Ah well,' smiles Joe. 'See you next year.'

As he leaves the rock behind,
There's a doubt in Sidney's mind.
'Something else I had with me . . .
Let me think. What could it be?'

Sidney gets home late that night.
His neighbour calls out: 'You all right?
Trip go well? Enjoy the sea?'
'Fine,' he says. 'But where's my key?'

For Toby and Thea P.R.

KESTREL BOOKS
Published by Penguin Books Ltd, Harmondsworth, Middlesex, England
First published 1984

THE VIKING PRESS
First published in 1984 by The Viking Press
40 West 23rd Street, New York, New York 10010

Published simultaneously in Canada by Penguin Books Canada Ltd

Text Copyright © 1984 by Paul Rogers
Illustrations Copyright © 1984 by Celia Berridge

UK ISBN 0 7226 5870 2

Library of Congress Cataloging in Publication Data

Rogers, Paul, 1950 –
Forget-me-not.

Summary: A forgetful lion loses his possessions one by one during a trip to see a friend.
[1. Lions – Fiction.   2. Travel – Fiction.   3. Lost and found possessions – Fiction.   4. Stories in rhyme]
I. Berridge, Celia, ill.   II. Title.   PZ8.3.R67Fo   1984   [E]   83–5969
US ISBN 0–670–32365–9

Printed in Great Britain